The Grey Ghost

Written by Stuart Hill

Illustrated by Maria Brzozowska

Collins

Chapter 1

I sit gazing out of my window while the sounds of
the early night fill my room. Jackdaws gather, calling
and squabbling as they settle to roost. Nearby, an owl
calls, its cry echoing over the still sky. Many people
believe night air is bad for your health, but I've always
slept with my window open. I like the night's soft
sounds to fill my senses as I lie in bed.

I live in Bradgate House in the Shire of Leicester.
It stands in the middle of the countryside, and because
the land is too stony and poor for farming, it's been
left wild. Between the oak woods, wide patches of
bracken hiss and sway like the sea when the wind
blows through it. But tonight there's only a gentle
breeze and the world is draped in the soft grey light
of the moon, turning the world to silver and shadows.
Nearby, the stream that crosses our land babbles and
chuckles as it flows, filling the silent darkness with
its voice.

3

It's still quite early and I'm not yet ready for sleep. I shiver, not because it's cold, but because I remember what my personal maid, Elizabeth Woodley, said earlier about this being the season of ghosts. The days are growing shorter, allowing the night to fill the world with shadows and mystery, and Halloween is just a few weeks away. There are many legends connected to this time. Some of them are known throughout the land and some are local. One story tells of the Ghost Pack – wolves that died long ago who run through the night, hunting down those who have not yet reached the safety of home. It's said that if they detect your scent, they'll

chase you through the darkness and tear you to pieces. I love these old legends – I know they're all nonsense, of course; there are no such things as ghosts, but they make wonderful stories.

My name is Jane Grey, a simple name – you might even say a plain name. But I am the great-granddaughter of one king, and the cousin of another. My father is Henry the Duke of Suffolk and my family are amongst the most powerful in all the land. So it could be said that just as a plain cover of a book can open to reveal an exciting story or beautiful pictures, my plain name hides the interesting facts of my family.

I continue to look out over the parkland that my family uses for hunting, containing red and roe deer. Sometimes we hold hunting parties, and many lords and ladies from the royal court come to take part in the chase. I don't like the hunting and killing, but at night there are parties, filling the Great Hall with colour as the lords and ladies dance, their gorgeous clothes shining and glittering in the candlelight.

My thoughts are interrupted as someone knocks on my door and Elizabeth comes in. She sees I'm in the shift that I wear to sleep in.

"Oh, Mistress, you're already prepared for the night," she says, as though annoyed with me.

"Well, yes," I answer. "But it wasn't difficult to get undressed by myself – I was only wearing my ordinary day clothes, not one of those court gowns with huge collars and impossible lacings."

Elizabeth is a local girl with dark chestnut hair, a square, determined chin and honest eyes. At 13, she's not much older than myself, but she's bigger and full of solid common sense – unlike me. I'm very well educated, and can read Latin, Greek and French, as well as calculate fractions and mathematics, but common sense isn't something I'm bothered with.

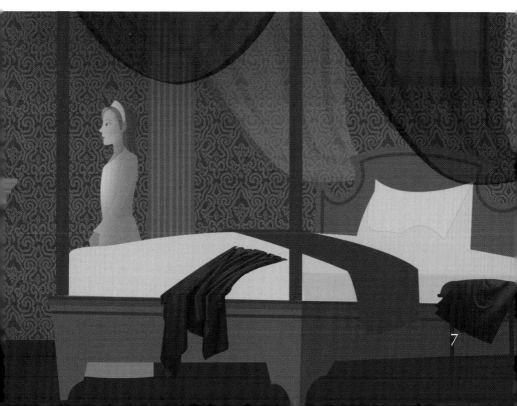

I wouldn't be able to look after myself if I was left on my own. I'd probably starve before I could work out how to make a meal or find water that's safe to drink! But why should I care about that? I am a cousin to kings, and I'm lucky enough to have been born into one of the foremost families in the country. Unless some unexpected tragedy happens, I'll always have people like Elizabeth to look after me.

I watch as she places the large jug and bowl of hot water for my wash on the nightstand next to my bed and smiles. "I'll just go and get you some clean linen."

"Oh, don't worry about that now," I say and pat the bed next to me. "Sit down and tell me a story about ghosts and spirits."

"And what makes my mistress think I know of such things?" she says, her nose in the air, trying to look like a haughty lady.

I poke her soft tummy to make her laugh. "You know lots of stories! You were talking about Halloween only this morning."

She giggles then and sits down. "Well, there is one tale I know." I'm surprised that her face gets suddenly serious. "It's actually a true story about my family and it's about this house and Bradgate Park too."

Elizabeth is a wonderful storyteller and I stay quiet, knowing this will encourage her to begin.

"This happened long ago in the time when my grandad was just a boy," she says. "A hunting party had been arranged and many lords and ladies came from the king's court to take part. My grandad, Ben Woodley, worked for your family as a gamekeeper, as did his younger brother, Edward. We all know that the Greys are an old and very important family, but in its own humble way my family is important too. We've been here since before William of Normandy came and killed Harold, the last Saxon king."

I'm surprised that Elizabeth knows history in such detail, but I say nothing and sit quietly while she continues.

"My people feel that they're not only servants to the Greys but also to the countryside. To this day we try to look after the land and keep it safe. We also try to protect the wildlife from being overhunted. But that particular hunting party long ago killed everything they could find: deer, and even hares and rabbits and the smaller animals. It seemed that they wanted to clean the park of everything that ran on four legs or flew through the skies."

Elizabeth is right about protecting the animals and land – I've seen some hunting parties that didn't seem to know when to stop killing.

"Well, my grandad and his brother took it into their heads to try to save some of the creatures," Elizabeth goes on. "They saw an exhausted deer being chased by the hounds and tried to herd her across the great stream that runs through the land just south of here. They knew the hounds would lose the scent if she went through the water. My great-uncle ran ahead of my grandad. He tore down the nets that the hunters had set up to drive and direct the deer towards open land, where they could be chased and killed."

12

Elizabeth pauses and I look out of the window on to the darkening parkland. For a moment I think I see a flash of white, as if some creature is running through the shadows.

But then Elizabeth continues: "Well, the hind ran through the hole he'd made in the nets and she made off over the stream. The hounds were following, but not close enough to see where she'd gone, and they milled about trying to find her scent. Then a great lord on a tall horse rode up and saw my great-uncle trying to put the nets up again. The lord guessed what had happened. He was so angry, he roared and bellowed at poor Edward. His horse reared, threatening to strike Edward down, but even that wasn't enough. The lord stabbed my great-uncle, killing him where he stood."

"But that's terrible!" I say. "Who was this lord?"

"I don't know. We never found out his name –
I suppose it was kept from us. But even if we had
found it out, it wouldn't have made any difference.
My great-uncle Edward was just a country lad and his
killer was a man of power, who was probably a friend
of the king's – he'd never have been punished for
his crime."

"But wasn't *anything* done?" I ask, angry at
the terrible injustice.

"Well, Lord Grey, your grandfather, did give our
family money to try to make some amends. He also
promoted the surviving brother, Ben, my grandfather,
to the position of full gamekeeper. But we suspect that
the king didn't want the killer to be harmed by any
scandal and so there really wasn't anything that could
be done."

I walk over to the window where I stand looking
out over the moonlit night. I don't know what to think.
Can any land ever be properly governed for the good
of everybody if the powerful can kill anyone and not
be punished?

"It all happened a long time ago, Mistress,"
Elizabeth says, joining me at the window. "I didn't
tell you the story to upset you. You said you wanted
a ghost story, and there's a mystery connected to
what happened."

"What do you mean?" I ask. Turning to Elizabeth, I'm hardly surprised to see her looking tense after telling me such a tale, but there's a sadness in her eyes too, almost as if the death of her great-uncle happened only yesterday.

"Well, you've heard of the legend of the White Deer that are supposed to haunt Bradgate, I suppose – " Elizabeth goes on.

"Yes, of course. They say that the white stag and hind are supernatural and that they come from the land of Faerie. It's all nonsense – only children and the uneducated believe in such things."

Elizabeth is quiet for a while, then says: "Yes, it's all nonsense. But not even an educated man like the minister will cross the park after the sun has gone down."

"Surely you exaggerate! Of course Reverend Jacobs doesn't believe in Faerie deer!" I say, not able to believe that a man of the cloth could be so superstitious.

"I don't know what he believes, Mistress," Elizabeth says. "But it seems the minister won't set foot in the park when the moon has risen, for fear of seeing the deer and the ghost boy."

"Ghost boy! Why would there be a ghost boy with the White Deer? Who could he possibly be?"

"There's a family legend that says it's the spirit of my great-uncle Edward, still a guardian of the land and helping to keep the deer safe in this world of mortals." A spark of fear gleams in her eyes. "After all, the White Deer come from the land of Faerie and it's said that the king and queen of that realm make bad enemies. If the deer are ever harmed, they could be angry. We all know that it's said the Faerie folk are neither good nor bad and sometimes they'll help people, but sometimes they'll turn against us and use their power to destroy our lives. Perhaps the ghost boy helps us all by protecting the Faerie deer."

I've heard these tales of the king and queen of Faerie many times before.

I'm about to say something about sensible people not believing in such nonsense, when a movement catches my eye. Something is moving over the land, something unclear, far off under the moonlight. I gasp, and for a moment, I think I can see two deer running and with them there seems to be a shape ... the figure of a boy running through the night.

A cold wind blows over us and I shake my head. "No, no, there are no such things as ghosts," I say firmly.

Chapter 2

The next day dawns bright and clear – it's one of those chilly, crisp mornings of early autumn that promises to be a warm day but starts with a frost and a delicious sharp scent of cold clean air.

I leap out of bed, determined to put the mystery and spookiness of the night behind me. After Elizabeth left me to settle down to sleep, my room seemed to fill with shadows, even though there were candles burning in the window. I kept telling myself that there were no such things as ghosts. My brain believed me, but my mind and imagination weren't convinced!

In the end, I had to give myself a good "talking to" as Elizabeth often says she does to some of the younger kitchen maids when they get cheeky.

In fact, I climbed out of bed and stood in the middle of the floor shivering in the draughts from the open windows. "Just you listen to me, Jane Grey," I said to myself. "You're a modern girl with the best education that money can buy, and let me tell you, that's a lot. Philosophers and thinkers say that ghosts don't exist, and if such intelligent people say so then it must be right. Now you just get back into bed and go to sleep and stop being so superstitious!"

I must say that I'm surprised just how much
I sounded like Elizabeth when I was telling myself off,
but she's one of the most sensible people I know, so
I suppose it's understandable. And it worked, because
no sooner had I slipped back between the sheets than
I fell asleep. But common sense doesn't seem to work in
the world of sleep and all night I dreamt of white deer
and ghostly boys who ran with them.

But now the sun is shining, filling my room with
brilliant light and driving out all my thoughts
of hauntings. I ring the bell and wait for Elizabeth to
arrive with my day clothes. I'm free today because my
tutor has to go into Leicester, the nearest big town, on
an errand for my father, so I'll be able to ride through
the parkland.

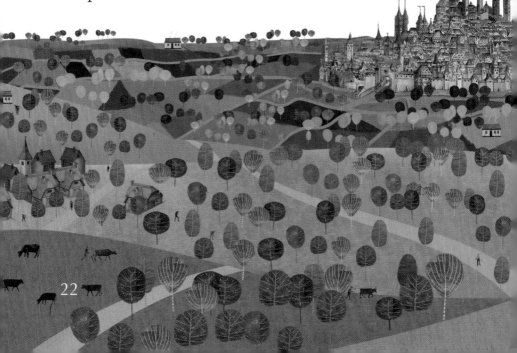

22

I have a beautiful horse called Matilda. It's a queen's name – fitting because my horse is very beautiful and very snooty. She's a well-bred palfrey, or riding horse. She's as black as night with a star on her forehead and a long, silky mane. And when she wants to gallop, she can outrun the wind! So it's just as well I've had the best riding masters to teach me how to control even the most stubborn animal.

A knock comes at my door and Elizabeth bustles in, full of energy.

"Oh, good, you're up already, Mistress. Well, I know you have no lessons today, so I've brought your riding things. It's a lovely day and a good gallop through the park will put roses in your cheeks."

"You've been reading my thoughts!" I say, with a laugh. "I thought I'd ride up to Beacon Hill and then on down into Ansty village. But I suppose you know that already, being a reader of minds."

Elizabeth pauses as she lays out my clothes on the bed that she'd just made in what seemed a matter of a few seconds. "Mind reader? No, not me – that was my great-aunt. She was accused of witchery and hanged when she told the local squire that the cottages he was having knocked down because they spoilt the view from his window would bring him bad luck. And they did too, because when the squire went to see how the work was getting on, a wall fell on him and broke his legs!"

I can't help laughing at this. "Is your family full of witches and ghosts, Elizabeth?" I ask.

"No, not really," she replies. "But perhaps more than some."

Elizabeth is too busy to stay with me after she helps me dress, and I quickly go down to the Great Hall for breakfast.

This is my favourite part of the house. Everyone eats here – from the poorest stable boy to my father, the lord of the household. There are three long tables that run down the length of the room where most sit, but I eat at the top table with the rest of the family. This table is made of solid oak and stands on a raised platform with a clear view down the length of the hall.

High above everything the hammer beam roof reaches across the wide space from one side to the other. Whole trees were felled in the local woodlands, then cut and shaped to make a wonderful weaving of arches and crossbeams. It looks as if an entire ship has been turned upside down and positioned on the walls to make a roof. I sit staring at this as I eat my breakfast of porridge and cold meat. Everyone else finishes eating well before me, so I quickly swallow as much as I can and hurry out to the stable yard before anyone can appear and find something for me to do that they think will be better than riding.

I arrive in the yard to find Matilda waiting with one of the grooms who will ride in attendance on me. No young lady is ever allowed to do things on her own – we always have to have a servant with us to act as chaperone. It's extremely vexing, especially when I'm only riding over my family's estate and know it better than almost anyone else.

To show how much I disapprove of these stupid rules, I climb into the saddle and immediately trot off through the yard without waiting for the groom to catch up. I clatter through the great gatehouse, down the cobbled trackway and on to the wide road that winds through the parkland. Then I suddenly urge Matilda to a gallop, and we fly along with the wind of our speed roaring in our ears.

The sun is still shining and the frosty grass glitters with rainbows, as though the Faerie queen has scattered her jewels over the land. The air is cold and fresh and I laugh aloud with excitement. I quickly look back over my shoulder and I can see the groom in the distance galloping to catch up with me. But I don't want to be caught yet, so I turn Matilda off the road and head for one of the many little woods that are spread over the estate like patches of green embroidery on a wide silken quilt.

I reach the edge of the wood and slow down so that Matilda can safely trot through the trees. At first the way is bright and clear, with shafts of brilliant sunlight thrusting down through the branches, but soon the trees become more and more crowded and the shadows deeper. It's almost as if a pool of night has gathered in the woods, hiding from the sunny day. The birds have even stopped singing and all I can hear is the soft sighing and whispering of the wind through the trees.

Matilda whickers and snorts nervously and I pat her neck to encourage her, even though I'm beginning to get nervous myself. It's odd, but now it's as dark as midnight, I even hear an owl hooting in the distance.

If I was superstitious, I could easily believe that some enchantment had altered time, and night really had fallen despite it being still early in the morning. Not only that, but I almost feel as if I'm riding through a strange forest instead of a small wood on my father's estate. The trees stretch into the deepening shadows all around me and I can see no sign of the edge of the woodland. I decide it's time to get back to the road, but just as I'm turning Matilda there's a sound in the distance. I sit listening and a shiver runs down my spine. It sounds like an animal howling.

The sound comes again, and this time it's nearer and other howling voices join with it. Could it be dogs? Or perhaps a pack of hounds out hunting? No, I know it can't be – only our hounds would be running over the estate and they're all locked up in the kennels. They'll already have had their daily exercise.

The shadows have got deeper still, and then suddenly two white deer burst into view only feet away! A stag and a hind and with them a running boy! My mind races – this is the first time I've seen the White Deer. I tried not to believe they were real, but now I can't deny it. They're real and they're running by me!

Matilda screams and rears. By the time I wrestle her down and get her under control, they've gone. But now the howling starts again and it's so close I expect to see a chasing pack running through the trees.

I peer through the shadows, and there they are. Long grey shapes, running close to the ground, with red eyes and lolling red tongues. In some ways they look like dogs, but I know they're not.

"Wolves!" I whisper to myself. But they're extinct in England. No one's reported seeing a wolf since the time of the old king's father more than 60 years ago!

Matilda screams again and the pack leader turns his red eyes on us. It's then that I realise what they are! It's the Ghost Pack of legend. An icy shiver of terror shudders through my body, but I know that if I'm to live, I have no time for fear! I urge my horse to a gallop and we hurtle through the trees. I crouch low in the saddle as hanging branches and twigs whip over my head. I manage to glance back and almost scream when I see the wolves are now chasing us closely and they're gaining on us!

I concentrate on guiding Matilda through the crowding trees. We can't fall now; the wolves would tear us to pieces. Then ahead of us, I see the deer and running boy again. Somehow, I know we must follow them, and we gallop on.

I'm losing all sense of time. We seem to have been running through the trees for hours, but I know this isn't possible. I look back and see the pack leader almost snapping at Matilda's heels. But now he gives a greater burst of speed and he's running beside me. I can clearly see his red eyes and the glittering whiteness of his teeth that seem to glow in the darkness. He leaps up at me and I strike at him with my riding whip. For the next few minutes, we struggle with each other – him leaping up with his gaping mouth, and me fighting him off with my whip.

Then the rest of the pack come surging up and they surround us. I can't fight them all! But at last I see the trees are beginning to thin and we burst out into the road and brilliant sunshine. The groom is just ahead and I shout to him. Matilda turns and rears, ready to fight, but she drops to the ground again, snorting. The wolves have gone and as I look back at the trees, I can clearly see right through the small wood to open land on the other side. Where is the dark forest? Where is the hunting pack?

The groom trots towards us looking annoyed and relieved. "There you are, my lady! I was getting worried."

Chapter 3

I don't say anything to the groom about the forest
and the wolves, but I do say that I think I've seen
the White Deer. He's a local man, so knows the legend,
and he nods, trying to hide a smirk. He doesn't believe
in ghosts and supernatural things during the hours of
daylight, like a lot of people, but I'm sure once it's dark
he'll think differently.

Now I have to decide what *I* think about these things. Only last night, I was telling myself that there are no such things as ghosts and white deer from the land of Faerie – and now I've seen them *and* a pack of ghost wolves! I can't wait to get back home and talk it over with Elizabeth!

We head straight back to Bradgate House, but when I get there and leave Matilda to be rubbed down and put back in the stables, my mother is waiting for me in the Great Hall.

"Ah, Jane!" she calls from where she's sitting next to the fire. "Come and join me." She stands and holds out her hands. She's very tall for a woman and towers over me as I walk up and take her hands in mine. Her hair was once blonde like mine, but now the few wisps that have escaped from her bonnet are silver. She nods to her personal maid sitting with her and the maid leaves us alone together.

"Now, as your tutor is away for the day, I thought we'd take the opportunity to practise some of the more *ladylike* skills that you really should know." Mother turns, takes up the embroidery she was working on when I came in and hands it to me. "Learning Greek and Latin is all well and good, but a true lady should also be able display talent as a seamstress and sing as prettily as a nightingale."

I feel my heart sinking down into my riding boots. I hate stitching and singing and all of the other things that young aristocratic ladies are supposed to be good at. I'd much sooner read about the Trojan War and Julius Caesar – or calculate angles and read maps of the countries beyond the shores of England!

"When did I last hear you sing, Jane? It must have been before Christmas. Give me a little song now – you can do it while you embroider."

So begins one of those horrible times when I have to behave like a lady. In fact, it lasts all day and I don't get a chance to escape until almost suppertime. But at last I manage to persuade my mother to let me go so that I can change into a proper dress, and I hurry off to my room.

When I get there, I find Elizabeth waiting for me. She knows I've been trapped all day and she smiles in sympathy as she dips in a quick curtsey.

"Was that tiring, Miss?" she asks, and her smile becomes a grin.

"More than tiring. I'm exhausted!" I say. "Who'd have thought that pulling a needle through cloth and having a polite conversation could take so much effort?!"

"Well, you're here now and don't have to worry about behaving like a lady anymore," Elizabeth goes on, helping me out of one dress and into another. "How was your ride this morning?"

I gasp as I realise that I haven't told Elizabeth about what had happened yet! I quickly take her hand and lead her over to the bed to sit while I tell her everything.

By the time I finish, her eyes are wide with excitement, mixed with fear. "Oh, Mistress! You've seen the Ghost Pack!"

"Yes, I know!" I say, gripping her hands tight in panic.
I still hardly like to believe in such nonsense, but I can't
deny that I've seen them. "I'm lucky to be alive. But are
they bad luck – a sign of doom or something?"

"No, not bad luck, as such," Elizabeth says.
"But they're not good luck neither. Legend says
the Ghost Pack haunt this world in search of souls."

"Well, they didn't get my soul; in fact, I beat the pack
leader around the head with my whip, so they know I'm
no easy prey!"

She laughs at this, her hands to her mouth and her eyes wide with horror and amusement. "Well done, my lady. The only thing is, they know your scent now and they'll be hunting for you again!"

As she says this, it's almost as though a cold hand rests on my shoulder, but I'm not going to admit I'm scared to Elizabeth. "Well, they'd better be careful because I still have my whip and I'm more than ready to use it."

But later, when I'm ready for bed, I close my windows on the darkness for the first time I can remember and I try to make sure my candles are lit all through the night.

I wake up when the moon has set and despite what I'd hoped, most of the candles have burnt out. My room is lit by one single flame that flickers and sends shadows dancing around the walls and over the ceiling. My eyes are drawn to my closed window and the darkness seems to press against the glass like the black paws of some nightmare beast. I try to be sensible and tell myself that even if it is a huge hairy creature like a bear or something, it obviously can't get in, otherwise I'd be dead by now. And with that I turn my back on the window and try to sleep.

Chapter 4

The weeks pass and I see nothing of the White
Deer or the Ghost Pack. It's almost as if I imagined
the whole thing. But then one day, Father and Mother
walk into the Great Hall and don't notice me sitting by
the fire, quietly reading about Julius Caesar and his
conquest of Gaul.

My chair is turned with its high back to the hall and
I stay perfectly still, hoping that I won't be seen and
made to waste my day doing "ladylike" things with
Mother again.

They're talking about something they've obviously
been discussing for some time.

"But how have these stories of ghosts and Faerie
deer reached the royal court?" my mother asks irritably.
"And why do they feel a need to come here to hunt
for them? Isn't it bad enough that we're haunted by these
peasant stories without the king learning we live among
such simple-minded people who believe these things?"

A hunt!? This is the first I've heard of anyone trying
to kill our Faerie deer! How dare they? I risk peeping
round the back of my chair and watch my parents as
they unhappily go on discussing the coming hunt.

My father's grey hair seems to glow in the shadowy hall, and because he's much shorter than my mother, he peers up at her with his eyes narrowed as if she's standing some distance away.

"I've no idea how the king found out," he says, "but the fact remains that a hunting party of some of the most powerful people in the country is about to descend on us with the intention of chasing the White Deer and killing them!"

"Such nonsense!" my mother says. "Well, I suppose we must prepare ourselves to bear the expense!"

I'm so angry about the idea of anyone hunting the deer that I could burst. I may not have believed in them a few weeks ago, but now I know they exist and I'm determined to try to save them. I hardly dare breathe in case I give myself away.

Then my father clears his throat and goes on:

"But at least the king himself has the good sense to stay away, which saves us a little money. If he had decided to come, we could have found ourselves spending more than our entire estate earns in a year."

Mother agrees in a flustered voice and at last they hurry off to begin preparations.

I sit and think carefully about what I've just heard. There'll obviously be lots of important lords and ladies coming to the house and there'll be feasts, parties and dancing. Something that I might have found incredibly exciting, if it wasn't for the fact that the only reason they seem to be coming is because the young men want to hold a night hunt in the hope of killing the White Deer. How horrible! Why do people need to destroy beauty? Why can't they just be happy in the knowledge that it exists?

Nothing much happens here in the countryside and visitors from the court would have been wonderful. But now all I can think about is how to stop them killing the deer.

I find out that they're due here next week and their outriders have already arrived to remind us to have everything ready, as if we need to be told how to behave!

✳✳✳

The visitors arrive early in the morning a week later, and what an exciting sight they make. Many of the gentlemen ride tall, fiery horses, as do some of the younger ladies, while others ride in a series of fine gilded coaches with an escort of ten mounted soldiers armed with spears.

I watch with the entire household as the procession clatters into our courtyard. Grooms hurry forward to take the horses, while Father and Mother greet them with an elegant speech of welcome. Maids and manservants guide the fine lords and ladies to their quarters to get ready for the ball that's to be held tonight. There are so many, it's been difficult to find room for them all, and their servants will have to make do with sleeping in the hayloft over the stables. Elizabeth and I retreat to my room where we discuss what we're going to do.

"The word amongst the court servants is that the hunt won't happen until after the ball, so we have time to prepare," Elizabeth says. "I've gathered together lots of different spices and strong-smelling things that could put the hounds off the scent. We could scatter them around any likely places the chase could happen."

"Good, and we can use my perfumes too,"
I say. "But I'm still not clear about the *nature* of
the White Deer. Do they leave a scent? Are they
physically real or are they just spirits?"

Elizabeth pauses. "I'm not really sure – nobody is.
Though some say that they live in both worlds and
when they come into our realm they have real bodies
and can be hurt. We have to help them back to the land
of Faerie where they'll be pure spirit and no one can
harm them."

I fall silent as I think this through. A few weeks ago,
I'd have laughed at such an idea, being a modern and
well-educated girl. But now I've seen the deer, I've seen
the pack of ghost wolves – I know they exist. All I can
do is go along with Elizabeth's plans.

The ball and banquet are everything I expected. The fine lords and ladies seem to glow in the light of the candles of the Great Hall, their brightly-coloured clothes glittering with jewels as they dance to the music of the minstrels.

But I can't relax and enjoy myself – I've arranged
to meet Elizabeth beyond the house walls just as soon
as the cry for the hunt goes up. And I don't have to
wait long for this to happen, because suddenly one of
the young men jumps up on to the top table, where
I'm sitting with Father and Mother, and blows a great
blast on a hunting horn. All the young men cheer
and scramble for the doors, and in the chaos, I slip
quietly away.

Chapter 5

The house and gates are usually locked up tight
by the striking of ten o'clock, as is normal in
the countryside where the working day starts so much
earlier than it does in the towns. Father insists on
calling it the "Curfew Bell" but actually it's the clock
of Saint Margaret's Church in the nearby village
of Newton. But with so many important guests from
the king's own court staying with us, our usual rules
are relaxed and all the gates are left unlocked. No one
would dare try to tell these London courtiers that
they're not allowed out after ten o'clock. The night
porter doesn't even take up his usual place in the lodge
by the main entrance.

This makes it much easier for me and Elizabeth to
sneak out without being noticed.

The moon's almost full as we open the small gate
in the wall that surrounds the kitchen garden. It's icy
cold and a frost glitters on the pathways like crystals
of moonlight. The night hunt set out a short time
ago – I don't think Father approved of a night hunt
but the king's courtiers can more or less do what they
please, no matter where they are.

An owl hoots nearby, and a fox calls. The air is still, with no movement of wind at all. There's a strong smell of wet earth and the first fallen leaves of early autumn. It's almost as if the night is holding its breath.

"It's quiet," I whisper, unnecessarily. Elizabeth nods and then grabs my hand. "Listen!"

In the distance I can just hear the yowling of hunting hounds following a scent. "They're heading this way," I say. "Quick, let's hide in the bracken!"

We hurry off the path and burrow our way deep into the thick stands of fern. The howling sound of the hounds gets closer and closer, but there's something wrong – I can't hear any horses. No hoofbeats, no excited whinnying.

"That's not the courtiers. But what else could it be?"
I ask Elizabeth, with a gasp of fear.

She shakes her head, the whites of her frightened
eyes glowing in the moonlight.

The howling draws closer, echoing over the night sky.
I go on, peering through the bracken, desperate to see
what it might be.

"The Ghost Pack!" Elizabeth screams in
sudden realisation. "They're hunting for souls!"

We hold each other as we stare through
the moonlit night. In the distance, there's a glow in
the sky and I think I can see huge wolves with red eyes
running towards us.

Closer and closer they come. Elizabeth grabs me
and we sit hugging each other in terror, waiting for
the Ghost Pack to catch us and tear us to pieces.

But then a great wind suddenly blows up and as it
calms again the White Deer step out of the shadows!

I cry out in relief, though I don't know why.
How could they save us? There's a proud antlered stag
and an elegant hind, and with them is a boy. They seem
to be made of mist and moonlight. They turn and stare
at the pack, as if they're deliberately trying to catch
and hold the wolves' attention. Then suddenly they leap
away, drawing the Ghost Pack after them.

"They saved us!" I say, almost weeping
with relief, as the pack disappear into
the night. "Elizabeth, the deer and the ghost
of your great-uncle saved us!"

"Yes, and now we've got to save them if
we can," Elizabeth says sensibly. "They can
run faster than any wind and should escape
the Ghost Pack. But they can't fight against
the hunt – with their nets and hunting
spears and the teeth of living hounds."

"Come on, then," I say. "Which way did
they go?"

"I'd guess down towards the stream that
runs through the estate. Legend says: if they
can get over that in the hours of darkness,
they'll be safely in the land of Faerie."

We run then, falling over boulders and
tree roots in the darkness, but soon we come
across a wall of high nets that must have
been set up earlier by the courtiers' servants.
The nets are there to stop the deer breaking
off in a different direction after the chase.
They wouldn't have much chance then,
unless they crossed the stream.

We scatter the strong-smelling herbs and spices, and my perfume, in the slim hope they'll put the hounds off the scent, and we also pull down as much of the net wall as we can.

We run to the stream. In the distance, we can hear the hunt approaching again. It's as though *we're* the quarry, as though *we're* being chased! We wade across the water to the far bank and then stop, uncertain of what to do. There's nowhere to hide – we're just waiting to be torn to pieces! But then we hear the light patter of hooves and what sounds like human footsteps … and suddenly the White Deer and the boy burst out of the darkness and leap across the waters to stand just a few feet from us.

Now the Ghost Pack appears from the shadows
and thunders down to the stream. They spot the deer
and howl and yelp in excitement. I close my eyes, not
wanting to see the kill.

But then I become aware of mist gathering over the waters. Elizabeth seizes my hand and points as it slowly writhes and billows. Eventually, it takes on the form of ghostly people who stand like a barrier against the pack.

Even so, the wolves still approach, their red eyes glowing as they move forward, their bellies almost touching the ground.

My eyes are then drawn to a point in the darkness close to where we're standing. We watch as two tall and elegant figures slowly seem to make themselves out of the shadows and night. Soon we're standing before what look like a man and a woman, both dressed in black, their clothes glittering with starlight and moonshine. I can't really be sure if I'm seeing the stars in the sky shining through their ghostly bodies or whether they truly are embroidered with sparkling gems.

Now the pack tries to cross the stream, their red tongues lolling and their howling filling the night. I scream, and the man and woman step forward. Power flows around them and they raise their hands to point at the Ghost Pack.

"STOP!" they command, above the howling of the wolves. "You have no authority here – you have no power! You will not stain our realm with your foul forms!"

The wolves skid to a halt and, as one, drop flat to the ground, cowering before the tall figures.

"Leave here and never again pollute our lands with your filth!"

The wolves yelp and grovel in the dirt.

"GO!" the man and woman roar, and the pack rises up and is swept away, tumbling and rolling like litter before a powerful storm wind.

Quiet now settles over the land. I can hear a vixen calling in the distance and an owl hooting on the hillside.

I gaze at the man and woman – at their crowns made of golden leaves and white flowers that glitter like diamonds, and berries that glow like rubies. I realise I'm looking at powerful monarchs.

Elizabeth grabs my arm. "Down on your knees – they're the king and queen of the land of Faerie!" she says, her eyes wide with both awe and fear.

The queen steps forward and smiles coldly at me.

She and her king are the beings that are neither
good nor bad. They didn't stop the Ghost Pack to save
us, they just didn't want such creatures on their lands.
It was just a coincidence that our lives were saved
by this. The king and queen will do just as they want,
and whether that helps people or hurts them means
nothing to them.

"Welcome to Faerie, Lady Jane Grey, soon to wear a mortal crown," the queen says in a voice that seems ageless, as if time means nothing to it.

"A crown?" I stammer. "Me? But how? I'm just a girl?"

"Even so, you will wear a crown," she says. "Though your reign as queen will be brief, even by the standards of the mortal world."

Then the tall king holds out his hand, and as his queen takes it, they both fade away into shadow and moonlight.

"But ... but wait ... what does that mean?" I shout into the empty night. An icy wind blows, cold as the grave, and Elizabeth puts her arm around my shoulders.

She turns us back to the stream and a movement
catches my eye. The deer and their boy are bowing
to us. With that they turn and bound away over
the moonlit land.

Everything now seems so empty and hollow.
We stumble our way back to the house and sneak
in through one of the many side gates in the wall.
But I can't shake off a strange sense of fear that follows
me back from the stream. What did the queen of Faerie
mean when she said I'd be a queen too, and why would
my reign be brief? I run over everything that happened
again and again, but I can't make any sense of it.

❋ ❋ ❋

The next day, the courtiers fill the house with excitement and energy as they discuss the night hunt, even though they saw and caught nothing. I stay in my room, still trying to understand what happened. Elizabeth appears with my breakfast and we talk about the night and the deer, but she doesn't understand either.

Later that same day, the courtiers leave for London. They seem as excited and happy as children let out of school early as they set off, bursting to tell the king about their hunt. No doubt they'll all invent stories of their great bravery and daring deeds.

The house echoes with emptiness after they've gone. I try to get back to a normal routine, but I can't. I try to talk to Elizabeth, but she seems to have changed. It's almost as if she knows something but can't or won't tell me what it is.

A month has passed, and I've seen nothing more of the White Deer or the ghost boy. It's quite late and as usual I'm looking out of my window over the dark land. Elizabeth knocks and comes in with my nightdress.

"It's cold, Miss. Perhaps you should close the window."

"Perhaps. I might close it later," I say, and then take her hand. "Elizabeth, do you still think about what happened on the night of the hunt?"

"Of course I do, Miss. How could I ever forget?"
She speaks brightly, but avoids looking at me, almost as
if she's embarrassed ... or even afraid.

"And you still don't know what the Faerie queen
might have meant about me being queen one day?"

"No, Miss. I'm just a simple country girl and such
high matters aren't for the likes of me. Perhaps
you need to talk to somebody who knows about
these things."

"Like who? No one who wasn't there could possibly understand," I snap, suddenly angry with the girl I once thought my friend.

"And neither do I understand. I can't say what the queen meant ... I can't even guess!"

She leaves, but pauses in the doorway, looking back at me. For a moment, I think I see a look of sadness on her face.

I turn back to my window and look out. The land seems to be made of silver and shadows and the cool late autumn air fills my room with the scent of fallen leaves and dying bracken. A flicker on the horizon catches my eye and for a moment I think I see white deer and the figure of a boy running under the stars.

A shiver runs down my spine at the sight, but then suddenly I feel my confidence returning!

It's nonsense to feel threatened by something that hasn't happened yet. I'm a young girl about to become a woman – I'm also the daughter of a powerful lord, the cousin of the king himself. And one day I will no doubt marry a man of importance and have children of my own, who will themselves be powerful and rule large estates and command the lives of many people. All my life lies before me, blessed by wealth and power.

What could possibly go wrong?

The legends of Bradgate House

The ghost pack

"Legend says the Ghost Pack haunt this world in search of souls."

The Faerie deer

"some say that they live in both worlds and when they come into our realm they have real bodies and can be hurt. We have to help them back to the land of Faerie where they'll be pure spirit and no one can harm them."

The ghost boy

"There's a family legend that says it's the spirit of my great-uncle Edward, still a guardian of the land and helping to keep the deer safe in this world of mortals."

The Faerie king and queen

"it's said that the king and queen of that realm make bad enemies. If the deer are ever harmed, they could be angry."

"She and her king are the beings that are neither good nor bad. They didn't stop the Ghost Pack to save us, they just didn't want such creatures on their lands."

Ideas for reading

Written by Gill Matthews
Primary Literacy Consultant

Reading objectives:
- draw inferences such as inferring characters' feelings, thoughts and motives from their actions, and justify inferences with evidence
- discuss and evaluate how authors use language, including figurative language, considering the impact on the reader
- provide reasoned justification for their views

Spoken language objectives:
- articulate and justify answers, arguments and opinions
- use spoken language to develop understanding through speculating, hypothesising, imagining and exploring ideas
- participate in discussions, presentations, performances, role play/ improvisations and debates

Curriculum links: History – A study of an aspect or theme in British history that extends pupils' chronological knowledge beyond 1066

Interest words: hurtle, surging, burst

Resources: ICT, books about Henry VIII and Tudor times.

Build a context for reading

- Ask children to look closely at the front cover illustration and describe what they can see. Ask when they think this story is set, where it is taking place and who the characters are.
- Ask children to read the blurb. Repeat the questions you asked about the front cover.
- Focus on the question in the final sentence and check that the children understand it. Ask what they think the answer to the question might be. Encourage them to justify their responses with reasons.
- Return to the front cover and read the title. Ask children what they think it means. Establish that it could have two meanings – a ghost that is grey or a ghost relating to the Grey family.

Understand and apply reading strategies

- Read pp2–8 aloud to the children. Ask what impression they have of Jane Grey. Discuss the relationship between Jane and Elizabeth. Ask if Jane Grey's name is familiar to them.